AMERICAN ACE

Also by Marilyn Nelson

Lyric Histories

My Seneca Village
How I Discovered Poetry
Sweethearts of Rhythm
The Freedom Business
Miss Crandall's School for Young Ladies & Little Misses of Color (written with Elizabeth Alexander)
A Wreath for Emmett Till
Fortune's Bones
Carver: A Life in Poems

Other Poetry Collections

Faster than Light: New and Selected Poems
The Cachoeira Tales and Other Poems
The Fields of Praise: New and Selected Poems
Magnificat
The Homeplace
Mama's Promises

Picture Books

The Ladder (translated from the Danish of Halfdan Rasmussen)
Beautiful Ballerina
Ostrich and Lark
A Little Bitty Man (translated [with Pamela Espeland] from the Danish of Halfdan Rasmussen)
Snook Alone

AMERICAN ACE

by Marilyn Nelson

Dial Books

DIAL BOOKS
An imprint of Penguin Random House LLC
375 Hudson Street
New York, New York 10014

I'd like to thank Solomon Ghebreyesus, William Timmins, and John Stanizzi for their helpful suggestions, and Jacob Wilkenfeld for his research on Connor's behalf. Thanks to the Air Force Historical Research Agency for their help in locating the photos used in the book. And I'll add here another shout-out of gratitude to my friend Pamela Espeland. —M. N.

Library of Congress Cataloging-in-Publication Data
Nelson, Marilyn, date.
American ace / by Marilyn Nelson.
pages cm
Summary: Sixteen-year-old Connor tries to help his severely depressed father, who learned upon his mother's death that Nonno was not his biological father, by doing research that reveals Dad's father was probably a Tuskegee Airman.
ISBN 978-0-8037-3305-3 (hardcover)
[1. Novels in verse. 2. Fathers and sons—Fiction. 3. Family life—Fiction. 4. Identity—Fiction. 5. United States. Army Air Forces. Bombardment Group, 477th—Fiction. 6. Racially mixed people—Fiction.] I. Title.
PZ7.5.N45Ame 2016 [Fic]—dc23—2015000851

Printed in the United States of America
1 3 5 7 9 10 8 6 4 2

Designed by Nancy R. Leo-Kelly
Text set in Adobe Jenson Pro

To the sons, daughters, and grandchildren
of the Tuskegee Airmen,
and to those who wish they were
their children or grandchildren

Table

Part One

Part Two

Part Three

Part Four

Part Five

of Contents

Part One

The Language of Suffering

My dad went weird when Nonna Lucia died.
It was like his sense of humor died with her.
He still patted my back and called me buddy;
we still played catch while the mosquitoes rose.
He still rubbled my head with his knuckles.
But a muscle had tightened in his jaw
I'd never seen before, and the silence
between us in the front seat of the van
sometimes made me turn on the radio.
I knew he loved his mom. We all loved her.
But when he smiled now, his eyes still looked sad,
all these months after Nonna's funeral.

Maybe there was some treasure he'd wanted,
that she gave to one of his brothers in her will?
Maybe he'd wanted some of the furniture?
But he got the embroidered tablecloth
Nonna and Nonno brought to America,
which she spread out at family festivals
under platter after platter after platter.
He wasn't a movie dad with another woman:
He was an oldish husband who'd just moved away,
a dad who didn't hear you when you spoke.
Me and Mom and Theresa could see his pain,
but we don't know the language of suffering.

Uncle Father Joe

One of Dad's younger brothers is a priest,
so we thought he could be the one to break
into Dad's silence: It's part of his job.
But he was so busy finding common ground,
preaching compassion, and working for justice
and human liberation that the small
curling-inward of his own big brother
got only his occasional hug, and prayers.
I couldn't ask, because I don't believe;
or don't know if I do. The difference
is moot, since anyway I've been confirmed,
like all half-Irish, half-Italian kids.

But Dad was spending another joyless night
sipping Chianti in front of the TV.
He looked like he might have been physically ill:
his face gray, his eyes lightless. He sat there
in his reclining chair sipping red wine,
letting Theresa control the remote.
Mom and I avoided each other's eyes,
each of us aching with mute, helpless love.
I went to my room and called Uncle Father Joe.
Do you know how depressed my father's been?
I asked. *Should he be on some kind of drugs?*
He said we should let Dad's mourning run its course.

Driver's Permit

Three months later Dad smiled a little more,
but that's the only improvement I could see.
Mom and Theresa and I tiptoed around
as if his silence was glass that could shatter.
Uncle Frank, Uncle Petey, and Aunt Kitty,
his partners in the restaurant business,
kept Mama Lucia's Home Cooking afloat.
They said the regulars were asking how Tony was.
Uncle Rich insinuated that maybe he should see a shrink.
Theresa whispered that Nonna Lucia
wouldn't have wanted Dad to take on so.
Nonna lived a good life. She was ready to die.

My half brother, Carlo, Dad's son with his ex,
who seldom visits, brought his wife and kids
to see their grandfather and cheer him up.
But nothing seemed to make much difference.
I googled *depression*. And I got scared.
A blue glacier was growing between us.
The melt started on my sixteenth birthday.
(March 17: St. Pat's. Mom's family
says it means I'm 51 percent Irish.)
Dad said I should get my driver's permit!
He promised me forty hours behind the wheel!
That was the best birthday present I ever got!

Hot Cocoa

Five o'clock Saturday morning: Dad's idea
of the safest time for driving practice.
It's pretty cool to be up and out together
while the day's still dewy and birdsong-y.
I got the hang of driving pretty quick,
except for the hyper-responsive brake pedal.
We drove around in my high school parking lot,
then drove aimlessly in the neighborhood.
At six o'clock Dad turned the radio on.
There was talk of illegal immigrants.
Dad mused about building a border fence:
To fence them out, or to fence ourselves in?

I told him we read a poem about that,
that I bet he would like, by Robert Frost.
Is he the one on the less traveled road,
with miles to go before he sleeps? Dad asked.
We read him in my eighth-grade English class.
I always wondered what the hell that guy
had promised, that made him stay on the road
instead of going home for hot cocoa.
I said, *My teacher thinks he was in love.*
And for the first time in a year, Dad laughed.
Behind the wheel with two lives in my hands,
I felt the wall between us start to fall.

Letter?

We've practiced entering the interstate,
changing lanes, speeding up and slowing down,
the turn signal, left turn against traffic.
I always feel like I'm driving around
two thousand pounds' worth of potential death.
Dad says he's glad to know I feel that way:
He says it shows I'm wise beyond my years.
We've been trying to drive an hour a week.
Depends on our responsibilities.
It's worked itself into a nice routine:
We listen to the radio, and talk
about whatever thoughts enter our minds.

It's funny to think about identity,
Dad said. *Now I wonder how much of us*
we inherit, and how much we create.
I see so much of your mother in you,
so much of Carlo's grandfather in him.
I used to love hearing I was like my dad.
Now I see that was just learned behavior.
I feel sort of like an adopted child
must feel, when he finds out he's adopted:
like he doesn't know anymore whose child
he is, like he doesn't know who he is.
And it's all because of the letter Nonna left.

Part Two

La Famiglia Bianchini

The Bianchinis closed the restaurant
on the anniversary of Nonna Lucia's death.
They held an over-the-top Bianchini feast
that evening. White tablecloths and everything.
Digital photos projected on a screen:
Lucia with two sons, then three, then four,
her face orbited by children's faces,
her beatific grief when Genaro died.
Uncles and aunts toasted the memory
of the woman who made them who they are.
I sat at the table of first cousins,
knowing Dad was going to break the bubble.

He clinked his glass during the spumoni.
Expecting a speech, everyone fell still.
He cleared his throat and said, *Mama left me*
a ring, a pilot's wings, and a letter
saying Genaro wasn't my father.
My dad wasn't my dad. My family
is only half mine. You're my half siblings.
My dad was an American, named Ace,
a man she loved with all her heart, who died.
Her letter didn't tell me his last name.
But my own last name is a deception.
I'm half Italian. I'm your half brother.

Chinese Gong

If someone had dropped the proverbial pin,
it would have sounded like a Chinese gong.
The Bianchinis rebooted Mama,
the girl before them, as a girl in love.
You could almost hear the noises their minds made.
They rebooted their papa, Genaro,
who worked long hours in the factory,
gray and stooped, with a beautiful young wife
and five children in whom he found much joy.
Then Aunt Kitty confessed she was a little shocked,
. . . but I'm glad to know Mama had a Grand Romance!
Tony, nothing makes you less my brother!

There were a lot of hugs among them.
And confusion at the children's tables.
One cousin asked, *Half of Uncle Tony*
is our uncle? So what about the rest?
Then Uncle Father Joe said, *In God's eyes*
all humankind is one big family.
Let us be grateful for the love we share.
Tony, I wouldn't be me without you:
You're as much Bianchini as I am!
There were a lot more hugs. There were wiped tears.
I wiped a few. Some were because I knew
one-fourth of ME was now an enigma.

Gold Class Ring

Mom patted Dad's hand on the steering wheel.
See? I told you they'd all feel as I do.
It's so romantic to be a love child!
I wish we knew who this American was.
Dad felt his parents had made him live a lie,
that their kept secret was a betrayal.
To think, he said, *whenever they looked at me,*
what they saw was my secret history.
He wouldn't share the letter, but he said
Nonna wrote he was the fruit of great love,
that Genaro's love had saved them both from shame,
and that his fathers would be proud of him.

In July, Italy won the World Cup.
Mama Lucia's Home Cooking was wild
with Asti Spumante, blaring music,
il Tricolore, men shouting *Viva!*
A conga line danced out on the sidewalk.
Some dancers were part of my family,
some were Italian people we all knew,
some were neighbors. All of them were happy.
The next day I drove Dad on country roads,
the interstate, and the lot at the mall.
After lunch he reached into his pocket
and put a gold class ring on the place mat.

Heirloom

It's too small for me. Can you get it on?
It fit the pinkie finger of my left hand
like it was made for me. I pretended
I couldn't get it off, then snarled and said,
You're mine at last, my Precious! and Dad smiled.
It's yours, then, Connor. Your grandfather's ring.
Maybe it's a clue to the mystery
of our inherited identity.
I said, *Mortal, beware of the power*
of heirlooms from the vampires' royal line!
I gave Dad a bloodthirsty, fangy grin.
Then I told him I'd use its power for good.

Hard to describe how the ring grew on me.
I looked at it hundreds of times a day,
admiring its rectangular logo
and the Latin phrase etched into the gold.
After some days, it belonged to my hand
as inevitably as my knuckles and nails.
It was PART of me. I understood what Ace
was saying when he gave Nonna this ring,
how much he loved the beautiful Italian girl
he probably talked to like "Michelle, ma belle,"
that McCartney/Lennon song on *Rubber Soul*.
My Nonna. She loved him for sixty-five years.

Italian Bling

I work at Mama Lucia's once in a while.
It makes people happy, and gives me some cash.
There's always a job to do in a restaurant:
for those who can't cook, there are always plates to wash.
So, I was there when three high-schoolish girls
took a booth at the height of the lunch hour,
and ordered three side salads and iced tea.
I poured their waters and one of the blondes
asked if she could get gluten-free croutons.
I tried to guess what her background could be:
Scotch Irish? Scandinavian? Polish?
The third girl was brunette, really pretty.

Italian, maybe, or Greek. Olive skinned.
The blondes were cute, too, in a different way.
I couldn't wait for my driver's license!
I turned away, but heard giggling whispers:
He's hot! Tall, dark, and handsome: Just my type!
I brought their food and lingered, ignoring
the disapproval of harder workers.
As I topped off their water glasses again,
the other blonde, with Atlantic blue eyes,
admired my pinkie ring. *Is it real gold?*
I smiled, nodded. As I turned away
I heard a whisper: *Italians love their bling!*

Part Three

The X-Factor

The next time I could get behind the wheel
the trees in the city were past blooming
and grown-up birds were parenting their young.
Dad guided me onto the interstate.
Okay, he said. *You drive; I'll navigate.*
I felt the engine's power, the road's rhythm,
the beckoning of the endless distance,
the beginnings promised somewhere out there
as time raced to the past under our tires.
The van was full of comfortable silence.
Once in a while the glint on my finger
reminded me to wonder who I was.

One-quarter of me was American:
Did that take me back to the *Mayflower?*
The ancestors I knew were innocent
of the white guilt of Indian slayers
and slave owners. Did this new grandfather
connect me differently to history?
I glanced at Dad. It must be worse for him,
to go from being 100 percent
to being half-American X-factor.
I signaled and moved to the passing lane
in front of a Harley I hadn't seen.
The biker swerved, and gave me the finger.

Baklava

H*e was going at least eighty,* Dad said.
With no helmet! Wherethehell are the cops
when you want them? He had a lot of nerve!
I was too shaken up to say a word.
Some minutes passed in silence. Then Dad said,
Let's get off here. I need to stretch my legs.
We pulled up in a farm stand parking lot
that announced fresh fruit pies and vegetables.
Another family was debating
whether they wanted a peach or an apple pie.
The saleswoman (was she the farmer's wife?)
was brown. A blue hijab covered her hair.

The apple pies are all homemade, she said,
with twinkling dark-lashed eyes. *I made them all,*
and I guarantee all are delicious!
A boy (seven, I guessed, and freckled) asked,
Do they have apple pies where you come from?
She smiled. *In Harrisburg? They certainly do!*
And, even better, they have baklava!
It sells out faster than the apple pies.
Next time you stop, I'll give you a free taste.
You'll love it! They bought peach, and drove away.
We bought apple. Dad promised we'd come back
to buy baklava for the restaurant.

Unknown DNA

It was Mom and Dad's regular Date Night:
Theresa and I ordered a pizza
and set up the schedule for the remote.
She had it first, but she wanted to talk.
Mr. Wisniewski, my science teacher,
says that if you're adopted, you should know
your birth parents' medical histories.
There are all kinds of problems you can have
if there's something wrong with your chromosomes.
What if our new grandfather had bad genes
and passed us some inherited disease?
Are you scared of his unknown DNA?

I told her I'd inherited a strong
craving to drink the warm blood of infants,
but since there were no infants in the house,
I'd settle for the blood of a twelve-year-old.
I lunged. She fought back with sofa pillows,
giggling her head off. When we settled down
I told her not to worry: Nonna's genes,
combined with all the Ryan and Malone
chromosomes, should provide a strong defense
against everything but stupidity.
She said, *I hope! But wouldn't you want to know*
if you're going to be totally bald?

The Stink Eye

We didn't drive as much when school started:
It was hard to synchronize our schedules.
But we made weekly Saturday morning drives
through neighborhoods, on interstates, in malls,
behind slow tractors pulling loads of hay
on little narrow winding country roads . . .
sometimes not talking, just bobbing our heads.
Once, driving aimlessly in the city,
I turned onto an empty dead-end street
of keep-out buildings with boarded windows.
I was performing a three-point U-turn
when three black dudes my age turned the corner.

Two were Will Smith–ish brown, about my height;
the third taller, more Derek Jeter–ish.
Under one arm he held a basketball.
Dad sat up straighter, and took a deep breath.
I put the car into reverse again,
again in drive, reverse again, then drive.
My U-turn added three or four more points.
It was embarrassing. And the black dudes
were laughing. But no one gave the stink eye.
Dad raised his hand as I stepped on the gas.
At the corner, I looked in the mirror.
They were executing a passing drill.

Suo Marte

We agreed to stop at Uncle Father Joe's,
which was only a couple of blocks away.
His midday Mass was probably ending,
and he always likes to make lunch for us.
As he boiled water and sliced tomatoes,
Uncle Father Joe asked Dad about the ring.
This is just the most amazing story,
Tony. Did Papa treat you differently?
Dad said, *I wouldn't have guessed in a million years*
that Papa wasn't my natural dad.
He called me "my beloved firstborn son."
He often told me he was proud of me.

Uncle Father Joe said, *And he WAS, too!*
Let's see the ring, Connor. I took it off.
It left a white line around my finger.
The Forcean, he read. *1940.*
Suo Marte. The initials MS. Josten.
He gave it back. *"Suo Marte": Latin:*
"By our own strength." I sure wonder who he was.
This is a mystery for Sherlock Holmes!
Sit. Bless our meal, and us to Thy service.
Mangiamo! Salad and carbonara:
I wolfed them down, inwardly promising
that I would learn what the ring had to teach.

Part Four

Dead-End Clue

For a couple of weeks, I studied it closely,
from every angle. I memorized its wear,
the depth of the engraving, each digit.
Inside, the word *Josten,* the initials.
My teachers must have thought I was obsessed.
Kids started teasing, calling me "Gollum."
My homies, Zach and Jonah, knew about
the mystery, so they cut me some slack.
But this cute girl, Amy, kept suggesting
I should give her my ring for safekeeping:
She'd wear it on a chain around her neck,
and keep it away from the Dark Powers.

One Date Night, after pizza, Theresa
and I googled *Josten* and *Forcean* for hours.
The Powers were definitely not with us:
Josten's a brand name; *Forcean,* a dead end.
We were so glum when Mom and Dad got home—
feeding our faces microwave popcorn
and drinking blueberry yogurt smoothies—
that Mom asked what was wrong. When we told her,
she said, *A good research librarian*
can guide you like thread through a labyrinth.
She said she'd take us to the library.

The Mystery Ring

Between classes, Amy kept showing up
near my locker, as if by accident,
blushing, dimpled, offering to keep my ring.
I think, in her mind, what she really meant
was we were starting a relationship.
Did I say she's cute? She's adorable.
But why was she drawn to me by the ring?
I started to feel like it had power:
It set me off, made me somehow different,
even though its meaning was still hidden.
I told her I couldn't give up my ring,
but I'd like to hang out with her sometime.

And thus began a beautiful friendship:
She came with me to the college library.
We talked to the research librarian,
then walked around the beautiful campus
until Mom picked us up and drove us home.
Three Saturdays led to the same dead ends,
but made Amy part of the family.
We were a new Bianchini couple,
brought together by "The Mystery Ring."
Finally, Jake, the research librarian,
pursued *The Forcean* to Google Books.
And then things started getting interesting.

The Forcean

Jake thought the ring might be related to
an unauthored book called *The Forcean,*
which was published in 1939.
The New York Public Library owned one:
He could order it through interlibrary loan.
He showed us a description of the book.
One hundred and twenty-seven pages.
Amy squealed, in a small library voice.
Jake grinned, then typed into his computer.
He said, *They'll lend it to the library;*
you'll have to read it here, in our Rare Books
Department. We'll have it here next Friday.

Theresa bounced up and down in her seat
as Amy and I described the breakthrough.
Mom smiled at me in the rearview mirror.
Oh, you guys, she said, *isn't this thrilling?*
What if Ace IS connected to this book?
What if he was an aspiring writer?
I know a couple of famous American poets
were military pilots during the war.
Let's hope this isn't another dead end.
In the backseat, my fingers and Amy's
interwoven pulsed like two hearts conjoined.
I knew *The Forcean* wasn't a dead end.

But

We all agreed that Dad should be the first
to see the book. We couldn't go Friday:
The mayor planned a dinner for his supporters
at Mama Lucia's. So, on Saturday,
we'd drive: to campus, around, then to lunch.
You know how time slows down when you're watching,
like watched water takes forever to boil?
The week was like ketchup at the bottom
of a bottle. Friday was molasses.
The dinner's four courses, dominated
by speeches, toasts, and kisses next to cheeks,
lasted past Mama Lucia's closing time.

Saturday morning, sleepy, out of sorts,
we set out early, to parallel park
on the business street next to the college
before we headed up to see the book.
Dad seemed too tired to talk, except about
turning the wheel, braking, and backing up.
After a while we parked on the campus
and walked across the quad to the library.
We found Jake in the Rare Books Department,
waiting. He said, *It's a college yearbook!*
It's for Wilberforce University!
But Wilberforce is an HBCU.

Historically Black Colleges and Universities

Jake explained: *An HBCU's a black*
college or university, from back
in the old days of segregated schools.
Dad took the book and sat down heavily.
He seemed to have had the wind knocked from his sails.
I sat beside him. He turned the pages.
THE CLASS OF 1939 PRESENTS . . .
Wilberforce, Ohio . . . Big brick buildings.
The president in wire-rimmed spectacles,
a distinguished pinstripe suit, a small mustache.
Faculty. Administrators. Clubs.
The *Forcean* staff. The graduating class.

Their names and nicknames, their activities,
their favorite quotes, and black-and-white photos
of young, earnest-looking college students
who would graduate into a world at war.
Fraternities, sororities, sports teams.
"Miss Wilberforce": brown, pretty, a cute grin.
"Miss Classic": ivory and elegant.
Collages of miniature snapshots,
stiff, uniformed groups of ROTC cadets.
And everyone in every photograph
was African American. Was black.
We read the ads. And then Dad closed the book.

Part Five

A Hundred *What-ifs*

Well, I'll be damned, Dad said. He tried to stand,
but something happened: He got his foot caught
between chair leg and table leg, I guess.
Anyway, he fell suddenly in a heap,
with a loud *OOF!* Jake and I helped him up
and sat him down again. He was so pale,
his sideburns and eyebrows looked black again.
My father may have been a colored man?!
We could see the book again the following week,
with new questions. For now, we shook Jake's hand
and thanked him. Then we hiked across the quad.
When we got to the van, Dad was panting.

Talk about "lost in thought." I turned the key
and pulled into traffic unconsciously,
my mind going a hundred directions
of *what-ifs* and *this means*. The first *what-if*
was what if this is just a red herring?
What if *Forcean*'s really something else,
and the Wilberforce yearbook is irrelevant?
My second *what-if* was what if it's right,
and Nonna's love was African American?
So Dad's biracial? Will this change our lives?
Dad's eyes were closed. He was kind of snoring
when we pulled up at Uncle Father Joe's.

What Families Are For

Four guys were in the rectory driveway
making good use of the basketball hoop.
Dad opened the passenger door and couldn't stand.
One of the guys cried, *Oh, my God! A stroke!*
Just like my Moms! He need a ambulance!
I ran around the car, but he caught Dad.

Dad stayed overnight, "for observation."
I waited with Mom, Theresa, Amy,
most of the uncles, some aunts and cousins:
Bianchinis there for Bianchinis,
illustrating what families are for.
That guy—his name is Antwan—stayed with us.

My half brother, Carlo, and I exchanged
some texts. He said they were praying for Dad.
Then the earth settled back on its axis:
Dad was okay! It was a false alarm!
But they would monitor his blood pressure.
He didn't talk much, after he got home.
He hadn't had a stroke, but he had had
a glimpse beyond. All of us had had that.
It makes you think, when somebody you love
looks Death in its steel eye. It makes you think.
Dad said, *Listen. This wasn't caused by shock.*
It was years of cannolis and that hike!

Googling *Wilberforce*

We spent our evenings googling. *Wilberforce*
led us to William Wilberforce, a great
British orator/abolitionist.
Amazing grace and philanthropic zeal
made Wilberforce champion chimney sweeps,
single mothers, orphans, and juvenile
delinquents, made him condemn cruelty
to animals. But he primarily
spoke of the misery and wretchedness
of the hundreds of stolen people chained
to each other in the holds of slave ships.
He won: England abolished the slave trade.

The university that bears his name
was founded in 1856, the first
HBCU in the United States,
its first students the mixed-race children
of rich, guilt-ridden Southern slave owners.
Plagued by financial insecurity,
tornadoes, and arson, it still survives,
welcoming students of all faiths, races,
and ethnic and national origins.
Its motto: *Suo Marte*: "By our own strength."
Ray Charles donated two million dollars
for a Music Department scholarship.

Lines of 0 0 0 0 0 0 0

The bare oak branches outside my window
scratched the screens like pets wanting to come in.
The moon's light was magnified by the snow.
Gray clouds scudded across like ocean liners.
I bent over the desk in my bedroom,
scribbling from margin to margin to hide
the poem I'd been writing about Amy:
O O O O O O O O O O O O O O O O O O O.
Love made every molecule of me smile
every time one of them thought of Amy.
Did Ace sometimes look out at the moonlight
writing poems about Nonna Lucia, his girl?

We drove to campus through mixed rain and snow,
behind a windshield smeared by wiper blades.
With Dad's new Handicapped parking permit
we parked near the library's main entrance
and elevatored upstairs to meet Jake.
The three of us studied *The Forcean,*
trying to figure out how to find Ace.
Jake said, *Maybe Ace is a cul-de-sac.*
(I asked him later: That means a dead end.)
Let's start with the initials M and S.
We can ask the Department of Defense
if the men we find have service records.

Ace

Jake said he thought Ace might be a nickname;
Nonna's Ace might be an aviator,
the victor in many aerial battles.
We know your Ace was a pilot, don't we?
Maybe he was a very good pilot.
Maybe he was a Tuskegee Airman.
You've heard of them, right? The famous all-black
fighter pilots in the Second World War?
I think the name's related to the wings.
Look at the junior class: They'd graduate
in 1940. Is there a junior
with the initials MS? More than one?

We'll send the DOD the matching names.
Maybe one was stationed in Italy.
We found Mozelle Scott (wide brow, close-cropped hair,
square jaw, straight teeth, large eyes something like Dad's:
Alpha Phi Alpha, Industrial Arts Club),
and Mannie Sparks (side-parted curly hair,
a trim mustache, eyebrows something like Dad's:
Omega Psi Phi, Wilberforce Players),
and Marvin Stallings (light enough to be
Sicilian, with a bright, confident smile
something like Dad's: Alpha Phi Alpha, Sphinx,
Varsity Basketball, Class President).

Part Six

Together in the Kitchen

I thought *wow* all the way back to the van,
and on the highway and the city streets.
I felt like a helium-filled balloon,
only the helium was the word *wow*.
Dad looked out the passenger-side window.
He said, *I'll have my DNA tested.*
It's possible this fiction isn't true.
Odd, that black blood should be invisible.
But everything in this story is odd!
He raised his eyebrows, shrugged.
That Mannie Sparks was a cool-looking cat.
I bet he swept the ladies off their feet!

He taught me how to brake without a skid,
and how to steer through one, if one happens.
We passed a couple of fender benders,
and heard ambulance and police sirens.
Hypnotized by snowflakes in the headlights,
I chewed my lip until we got back home.
We wound up together in the kitchen:
Mom, Dad, Theresa, and myself, chopping,
sautéing, stirring, setting the table,
discussing what we knew of history.
Theresa said, *Wow! Now I feel prouder*
of President Obama and Michelle!

Cringing

I was in my room doing my homework
when Amy texted that her family
would like me to come over one evening,
to meet. I gulped, then I texted back *k*.
The evening happened a few days later.
Emily, Mr. Grandall, and myself
sat sipping seltzer in the living room,
while Mrs. Grandall came and went with trays
of beautiful low-calorie hors d'oeuvres
she'd made with fat-free food equivalents.
Then we all sat down to eat brown salmon
with a green bean and mushroom soup side dish.

I know everybody's not Italian.
All families aren't families of cooks.
But I can't help noticing ruined food.
And nothing less powerful than Amy's
smile could have gotten me through that dinner.
Mr. Grandall saying, *We've had many*
garlicky feasts at Mama Lucia's.
Amy tells us it's your family business.
Mrs. Grandall saying, *Amy's told us*
you're part Italian, part Irish, and part—
um . . . something else you can't see.
I still cringe over the way I said *Yes*.

DNA

A few days later Dad got his results:
48% Iberian Peninsula
24% Great Britain
8% Ireland
7% Benin/Togo
6% Cameroon/Congo
4% Europe West
3% European Jewish
Well, I'll be damned, he said, shaking his head.
That's SIX more peoples, not just one or two!
So Ace connects us to the larger world!
Just imagine how all those peoples met.

We spent some evenings googling history,
caring about our people's sufferings,
taking pride in their arts and their triumphs.
It's like having more teams you can cheer for!
At school I felt like everyone should know
I'd become a citizen of the world.
Maybe the difference was only in me.
I walked between classes in slow motion,
seeing the ancient intertribal wars
still being fought, in the smallest gestures.
Little things I hadn't noticed before:
the subtle put-downs, silent revenges.

Thanksgiving Gasp

As usual, the Bianchinis had our feast
in Mama Lucia's private banquet room.
Uncle Frank and Uncle Petey were our chefs.
Four brothers and one sister—Aunt Kitty, the youngest,
who runs a hair salon, three children, and
her husband, Uncle Don, like someone born
with a title. Uncle Petey's a veteran
with PTSD, divorced, no children;
Uncle Father Joe's a Roman Catholic priest.
But the other Bianchinis were fruitful:
Dad's son Carlo was there, with wife and kids.
Plus Theresa, me, and eight first cousins.

A gas fire danced in the fireplace.
Our eyes sleepy with that post-turkey glaze,
we were still shoveling in the ravioli
when Dad clinked his water glass with his spoon.
In the silence he stood and cleared his throat.
Before the pie, I'd like to share my thanks
for what Connor and I have learned from the ring and wings
my father left with Mama, and Mama left me.
Apparently, Ace was just his nickname,
earned as a crackerjack fighter pilot.
(Applause.) *And he was African American.*
He may have been a Tuskegee Airman.

Now That We're Colored

One evening a few days after Thanksgiving
Dad's phone rang. We were clearing the table.
He sat down. We kept working around him.
Hey, Carlo! You still eating leftovers?
Great to have you and the grandchildren here!
What? My goodness, Carlo . . . Sorry, son . . . Wait!
Dad looked at his phone, then he looked at Mom.
He says bad news should be told privately.
He should have known before the family.
He would have liked to tell his kids himself.
One of his kids asked, on the drive back home,
"Will we still have friends, now that we're colored?"

"Now that we're colored." Dad repeated that.
Over and over, in the next few days,
he'd look up from something, and look at us.
At school it was time for final exams
and decisions about spring semester.
I'd decided to write an honors thesis
on what I could find out about our Ace.
I told Dad as I steered through snow flurries,
concentrating hard on the road ahead.
When he responded, his voice sounded slurred.
I turned, asked *What?* His face was lopsided.
I drove straight to the emergency room.

Part Seven

Acute Care

Discovering the Tuskegee Airmen
Submitted by Connor G. Bianchini
for U.S. History Honors

Handsome black men with white in their eyebrows,
they stand, or sit at attention in wheelchairs,
saluting Old Glory, watched by a mixed crowd
of multiethnic young'uns who don't know
the half of what they went through to serve her.
In aviator glasses, red blazers,
and military insignia caps,
with lifted elbows and unbending backs,
they watch their flag progress, remembering.
We see them on TV, and at local
parades: heroes of a long-ago war,
celebrated for being Negro firsts.

Ho-hum, we think. *How many veterans*
are going to turn out this Fourth of July?
How many wars will be represented?
But the Tuskegee Airmen are different.
Theirs was both heroism in action
and inward heroism, where they fought
to prove themselves moral superiors
to institutions and shortsighted men.
It's a historical phenomenon:
Victims finally defeat oppressors.
In the struggle of whose rights and who's wrong,
economics finally lose to ethics.

Rehab

Add what you learn in twelve Februarys
to what you've learned about the 1 percent.
Now, close your eyes and imagine Master
whipping an enslaved man with a bullwhip.
To understand the Tuskegee Airmen,
you have to add up a lot of stuff like that:
the years of slavery and of Jim Crow,
the tricks of finance, unequal laws,
the notion that blacks are inherently
inferior. The army studies finding
Negroes to be "barely fit for combat."
The U.S. Army Air Corps being all-white.

In 1941, Yancey Williams,
an HBCU student, sued to join
the U.S. Army Air Corps.
So the army started a segregated
unit to train black pilots and ground crews,
at Tuskegee (tus-KEE-gee), the HBCU
founded by the great Booker T. Washington,
famous again every February.
Yancey Williams was the first Tuskegee
air cadet, first in the experiment
testing if Negroes can be taught to fly.
The Negro airmen aimed to prove they could.

Daily Visits

Their name for themselves was Lonely Eagles.
Their commanding officer's story suggests why.
Colonel Benjamin O. Davis Jr.,
son of the first black general in the army,
was the first black general in the air force.
At thirteen years old, he was allowed to fly
with a barnstorming pilot. That first thrill
of noisy soaring showed him his future.
After the University of Chicago,
he won a nomination to West Point
(from the only black U.S. Congressman),
which he entered in 1932.

The lone Negro cadet, Davis was shunned.
Nobody spoke to him, or roomed with him,
or ate or studied with him, for four years.
This silent treatment made him determined
to graduate at the top of his class.
He was thirty-fifth of two hundred seventy-eight.
Rejected for the air corps (no blacks allowed),
he was assigned to an all-black regiment
and not allowed into the officers' club.
To avoid having him command white men,
he was sent to Tuskegee to teach ROTC.
He was there when Tuskegee Field opened.

Watching Dad Come Back to Life

There were big stories in the Negro press.
(Some of their names: the *Pittsburgh Courier,*
the *Chicago Defender,* the *Amsterdam News,*
the *Bay State Banner,* the *Cleveland Call & Post.*)
Their headlines read *"NEGRO PILOTS GET WINGS."*
Their stories answered *who, what, where,* and *when,* but *why*
was answered in the hearts of 10 percent
of America, men and women newly proud.
Photos showed scenes from the pilots' lives:
A white colonel pins wings on the jackets
of five black lieutenants, members of
the graduating class of Negro Firsts.

Cadets stand at attention for review:
the head erect, face straight, the chin drawn in,
arms straight, the fingers curled so the thumb tips
just touch the first joint of the forefingers,
the legs straight, but without locking the knees,
the heels together, with the toes forming
a 45-degree angle in shoes
polished until they are leather mirrors.
Cadets, seated, "eat square" in the mess hall,
with their backs a fist's distance from the chair,
both feet flat on the floor, lifting the fork
straight vertically, then straight into the mouth.

Reading Dad the Headlines

Connie Napier saw a lynching as a child.
His great-grandfather was a Cherokee chief.
He made model airplanes, studied physics.
His after-school job bought flying lessons.
He soloed as a sophomore in high school.
A straight-A student and a star athlete,
he tried to volunteer for the air corps,
and was rejected, based on black incompetence.
He begged to be examined. Told he had failed,
he asked to be retested in two weeks.
This time, they said his score proved he'd cheated.
He wrote to the President, and got in.

One day, flying out of Tuskegee Field,
his P-40 sputtered and spat black smoke.
He landed in a ripening cotton field:
rows and rows of green plants with round white eyes,
being picked by prisoners in a chain gang.
Fifty black men in black-and-white-striped suits
and striped caps, dragging long, black cotton sacks,
stared at him, round eyes white as cotton bolls,
teeth-missing mouths wide with astonishment.
He stopped, his prop raising a cloud of dust.
Ignoring the white guards with their shotguns,
he grinned and saluted the prisoners.

Part Eight

Holding Dad's Juice Glass

Southern congressmen tried to cut the funds,
to kill the new black program on the vine,
to keep blacks on the ground where they belonged.
But First Lady Eleanor Roosevelt
went to Tuskegee, demanding to be flown
by a black pilot. Photos hit the news
of Mrs. Roosevelt in a Piper Cub,
wearing a flowered hat and a big grin,
piloted by smiling Chief Anderson,
the nation's first Negro licensed pilot.
The Tuskegee Army Air School breathed again,
its first class the 99th Pursuit Squadron.

After training, their deployment was stalled
for months, until they were finally sent
to North Africa in 1943,
to fly secondhand P-40 aircraft.
Attached to a previously white unit,
the 99th pilots were limited
to ground attack: They were ordered not to engage
in air-to-air combat. Then they were criticized
for failing to attack, for cowardice.
Southern congressmen threatened to disband
the squadron. It was moved to Sicily.
There, it earned a Distinguished Unit Citation.

Feeding Dad a Salisbury Steak Dinner

Tuskegee graduated more pilots;
the all-black 332nd Fighter Group
with three squadrons was sent to Italy
in 1944. The 99th
was assigned to this group, under the command
of Colonel Benjamin O. Davis Jr.
Equipped with P-47s and P-51s,
they painted the tails of their aircraft red,
and thus became known as Red-Tail Angels.
From Ramitelli field they flew escort
for bombing raids into Nazi strongholds
as distant as Poland and Germany.

Of almost two hundred bomber escort missions,
the 332nd lost significantly
fewer bombers than other fighter groups,
and shot down a hundred and twelve enemy planes.
None of them shot down five or more, so none
were actually "aces," but ninety-five
were awarded the Distinguished Flying Cross.
On one spring day in 1945
Colonel Davis and his Red-Tails escorted
B-17 bombers to their target,
a heavily defended tank factory in Berlin.
On that day they shot down three German jets.

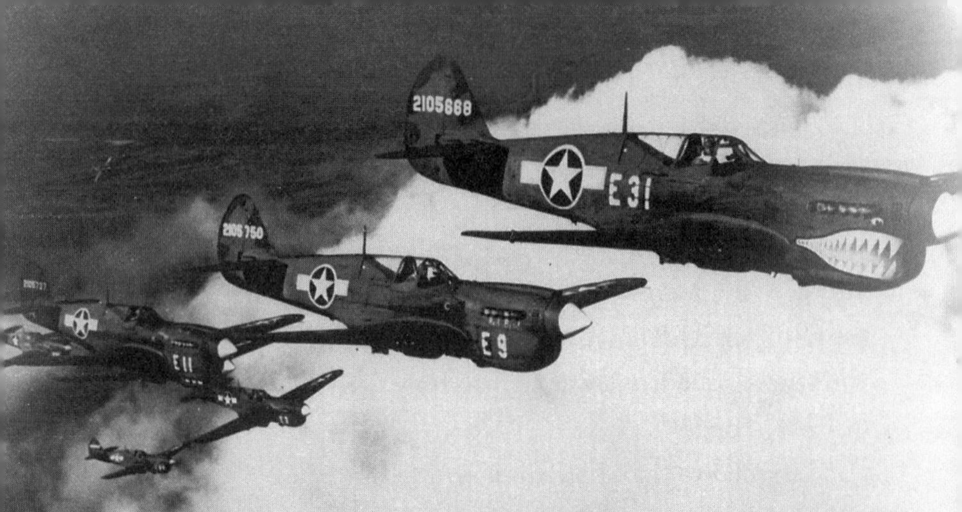

Wheelchair to Walker

The pilot gets up at 6:30 and packs his stuff,
shooting the morning's bull with his tentmate.
If he misses breakfast, he'll feel starved by noon,
so he drinks the powdered coffee, eats powdered eggs.
At 8:00 they'll be briefed for an escort run
to Turin, maybe, with B-17s
and B-24s, to bomb the railroad yards.
Whenever enemy fighters show up—
Messerschmitts and Focke-Wulfs—
the white pilots chase and get victories,
but they hang tight as ordered, and bring in
all of the bombers unblemished as newborns.

They leave Turin's railway twisted debris
and fly to refuel at the base on Corsica,
looking down on green peaks, cliffs, the moving blue.
It hurts to see a crash. But *c'est la guerre,*
he thinks. *Thank you* would be his constant prayer,
especially boots on the ground and belly full.
With luck, this will be an ordinary day,
one of a series of days that will keep him safe,
and will take him home to a long, happy life.
With luck, he will not fall spiraling from the sky.
With luck, he will live to hold his grandchildren.
He lies on his cot, thinking about luck.

Rehab Christmas

On a plate-glass-window, ceiling-unlimited morning,
a squadron of Mustangs scrambles into the sky
to a rendezvous at twenty-five thousand feet
over Umbrian villages and the lie of peace.
Despite his sheepskin jacket, Lester shivers,
more from anticipation than from cold.
The pilots of the bombers he's escorting
might refuse to shake his hand, but what the hell:
Homefolk Chicago teachers write to him
and send kids' crayon drawings signed with love.
Black dots emerging from blue clarity
develop into Messerschmitt 109s.

Lester approaches to two hundred feet,
thumbing his fire button to release
an *ack-ack* burst of steel. The Hun explodes.
A second Hun buzzes in at three o'clock.
Lester banks right and fires. A tail of smoke
follows its spinning dive. A parachute
blossoms at seven thousand feet. A third
bandit shoots gray lines past him. Lester chops
his throttle, falls behind, and fires a burst.
The Hun rolls upside down, screaming toward green.
The brothers radio verbal high fives,
regroup around the white boys, bring them in.

Moving Dad Home

Meanwhile, here in America,
the Army Air Force established a new
unit: the 477th Bombardment Group,
comprised of pilots, gunners, and bombardiers,
to be deployed in 1944.
The 477th was stationed at Freeman Field,
Indiana: four hundred black officers.
But they weren't allowed into the officers' club.
Ordered to sign papers saying they understood
the officers' club was for white officers,
they refused. Their sit-in termed a mutiny,
they were arrested and court-martialed.

The 477th was inactivated,
then integrated with the 99th,
returned from Europe. Under the command
of Colonel Davis and other black officers,
the new 477th Composite Group
was ready to go, when the war ended.
Of nine hundred ninety-two Tuskegee pilots,
three hundred and thirty-five were deployed,
sixty-eight of them were killed in action,
and thirty-two of them were prisoners of war.
In 1948 President Truman
integrated the U.S. Armed Services.

Part Nine

Beginning

Dad was released on Theresa's birthday.
She'd planned a bowling party with ten girls.
We welcomed Dad with undiminished joy,
followed his walker to his favorite chair,
and took our usual seats around the room.
Mom said, *Tony, my love, we're all so glad
to have you home again. Thanks for solving
Theresa's dilemma. We'll be back soon.*
She grabbed her keys; they left. And me and Dad
sat there. For me, the last few months a blur
of school and Amy, the most vivid hours
were those I'd spent in Dad's semiprivate room.

The hours I'd spent watching Dad mend his brain:
they were the only ones that held meaning.
Those, and the hours I'd spent discovering
the Tuskegee Airmen, that brotherhood
of brothers. One of them was shot down twice,
escaped twice from a POW camp,
and walked home to their base in Italy!
They were heroes of determination.
I'd seen that determination in Dad.
The doctors said he was very lucky.
But it could be that you make your own luck.
Shot down twice, caught twice, but free and walking!

The Floodgates Opened

We both said, *So . . .* at the same time. We laughed.
I said, *You're home.* Dad said, *So, how's Amy?*
I shrugged. *She might or might not be the one.*
Dad nodded. *Time will tell. And there's no rush!*
I filled the pause with trivial questions:
Could I bring him something? Make him some tea?
Did he want to see if there's a game on?
I didn't know why it felt so awkward.
We, who'd stood side by side looking at death.
How are your Tuskegee Airmen doing?
Have you made much progress on your paper?
It was as if he'd opened the floodgates!

I told him about the eager volunteers
who rushed to enlist as soon as the news went out
of the Tuskegee Air experiment:
Men came from all over America,
some from so far west they had never known
another Negro family—or hate.
Some came from high school, and faked their ages;
some were Ivy League grads; from the Midwest,
the South, from the Northeast: A thousand men
pledged they would fight or die for their country.
The way they were treated makes me ashamed.
But the way they treated others makes me proud.

Heroes

We talked 'til he got tired. I helped him to bed.
I ate a slice of Theresa's birthday cake,
when she and Mom got home. And the next day
there was a letter from the DOD.
Mozelle Scott and Mannie Sparks had both served,
Scott in the 99th Pursuit Squadron,
Sparks in the 332nd Fighter Group.
So both of them were Tuskegee Airmen,
both stationed in Italy. One shot down,
one crashed when his landing gear malfunctioned.
Black warriors. Potential grandfathers.
Imagine: Heroes in our family!

An almost faceless African American dude
in a leather helmet and big goggles,
a white silk scarf framing his jaw and chin,
soft, warm brown eyes that could freeze to a steel gaze:
a grandfather anyone would hope for.
And my warrior father, giving death
the finger as he fought to bring the lights
back to the stroke-darkened parts of his brain:
He was a hero in the family, too.
Whoever Ace was, Dad was my hero,
pushing himself forward for love of us.
Strong, defiant, courageous.

DMV

Dad thought I should get my driver's license.
I'd been driving Mom here and there for weeks;
he thought I'd been practicing long enough.
We waited three hours at the DMV
as a cross section of America
entered, waited, was called to the counter.
I aced everything, from the written test
to parallel parking. And I looked cool
and hot at the same time, in the photo.
We'd been invited to Uncle Father Joe's.
The muddy vestiges of the last snow
made puddles we splashed through as we drove there.

In the car, I told Dad about Ed Gleed:
how he was briefly Bing Crosby's chauffeur,
and then Bob Hope's butler, how he was first
in the first cadet class to graduate,
and how he'd shot down two enemy planes.
We pulled up at the rectory. Two guys
stood there talking with Uncle Father Joe.
One of them was Antwan. They helped Dad out,
and walked him and his brother to the door.
Antwan and I slapped palms, bumped fists, and grinned.
This here's Jameel. Jameel, this here's Connor.
Antwan bounced the ball and passed it to me.

Beyond Skin

You'd hardly notice that Dad drags one foot
and sometimes sort of wobbles toward one side.
I got an A on my honors thesis.
Amy's been dropping hints about the prom.
Antwan's working at Mama Lucia's.
I see him there a couple of times a week.
I'm trying to save some money for a car.
Inside, I'm both the same, and different.
I'm different in ways no one can see.
For instance, when I see or hear the news,
I think now, *Yeah, but what about the poor?*
Hey, what about the people of color?

I feel like there's a blackness beyond skin,
beyond race, beyond outward appearance.
A blackness that has more to do with how
you see than how you're seen. That craves justice
equally for oneself and for others.
I hope I've found some of that in myself.
Theresa and Dad and I agree that we're proud,
though we don't claim to "be" African American,
or brag about "our" Tuskegee Airman.
Unlike Carlo. He says it's God's best joke
that a white man like him could have black genes,
and that polenta's still better than grits.

How This Book Came to Be, and Why an Older African American Woman Ended Up Writing as a Young White Man

My father, Melvin M. Nelson, was a captain in the United States Air Force, a navigator, and one of the Tuskegee Airmen, the first African American military aviators in the U.S. Armed Forces. I have long wanted to write a book about the Tuskegee Airmen for young adults, and when I suggested it to my editor, she said yes—but write it for readers who know nothing about the Tuskegee Airmen. Write it from the point of view of someone who's learning about them for the first time.

Some people believe that young adult readers can only identify with young adult characters. I'm not convinced this is correct, and if it is, it might be something writers and teachers and editors should try to change. But I decided I needed a young adult protagonist—a central character other young adults would be comfortable reading about. And here came my first big challenge: Who would this character be?

The story of the Tuskegee Airmen is an African American story and an important piece of twentieth-century African American history. Most African American young adults have heard about them during February, Black History Month. (At least, I hope they have.) Tuskegee Airmen in their red blazers attended President Obama's inaugurations and appeared on television. So I couldn't imagine telling the Airmen's story as a young African American adult who was totally clueless about them.

I wondered—could I move the story into the past? Could the protagonist be the younger brother of a Tuskegee Airman, or years later, a Tuskegee Airman's son? I couldn't imagine how or where to begin.

Then I remembered the furor I'd seen on Facebook after the 2012 release of *Red Tails,* George Lucas's movie about the Tuskegee Airmen. There was a lot of chatter about the fact that the only love story the movie told was a fantasy about one of the African American pilots and a beautiful young Italian woman. My African American Facebook friends wanted the love story to be between a pilot and the African American girl he'd left behind. I don't think that would have been very dramatic: A movie about the exchange of love letters would be boring! And, since the Airmen were stationed in Italy, it's possible that one or two of them might have been involved with Italian girls.

I don't know of any such romances, but one of my childhood friends, Brigitte, was a biracial girl born in 1946 to an African American soldier father and a German mother. The mother gave her away at birth, and she was adopted by a childless Tuskegee Airman and his wife.

Recent genealogical and DNA research tells us that a large percentage of so-called "white" Americans unknowingly have African American ancestors. According to Professor Henry Louis Gates Jr. of Harvard University, the percentage of self-identified white Americans whose DNA is at least one percent African is, in some Southern states, as high as twelve percent.

I thought it might be interesting to imagine a Euro-American family's discovery that they are also African American. I remembered reading a powerful novel by Sinclair Lewis when I was a young adult. Published in 1947, *Kingsblood Royal* tells of a middle-class Euro-American man in a small Midwestern town who learns that one of his forebears was a famous African American explorer. He is delighted, proud. But when he tells his white friends, they snub him and rub his nose in the nastiness of racism. At the novel's end, he and his few new black friends are barricaded in his house as his white neighbors march toward it with guns and torches.

I thought the Italian American grandson of a Tuskegee Airman might not know anything about the Tuskegee Airmen, but that an interest in his own family history might ignite his curiosity and make him identify with the history he discovered in his research. And now I had my protagonist.

I remembered my father's class ring, which I always hoped I would inherit (instead, it was given to my younger brother, who told me years later that he gave it to some girl he liked in high school, whose name he no longer remembered). The ring takes on another life in this story. I did inherit my dad's college yearbook. He went to Wilberforce. The yearbook also plays a part here.

Many writers travel through a labyrinth of thinking to arrive at a story, a protagonist, and finally a book. My labyrinth led me to invent Connor Bianchini and his grandfather. I did not invent any of the facts Connor learns about the Tuskegee Airmen. That part of the story is true. And still amazing.

About the Author

Marilyn Nelson is a three-time National Book Award finalist, has won a Newbery Honor, a Printz Honor, several Coretta Scott King Honors, the Commander's Award for Public Service from the Department of the Army, and several prestigious poetry awards, including the Poets' Prize and the Robert Frost Medal. She has also received three honorary doctorates. She lives in eastern Connecticut.